Tied to the Carolinas

ॐ

Christine MacLeod

Tied to the Carolinas
Copyright © 2022 Christine MacLeod

Comments prosencons@live.com

Cover Photo
Courtesy of Austin Bond

ISBN:
978-1-950768-83-7

Published by Prose Press
Pawleys Island, SC 29585
prosencons@live.com

*This book is dedicated to
the matriarch of a
beautiful family.*

Forward

Love…my favorite four letter word. You can wish for it, pray for it and want for it, but it will elude you until you are ready for it. We spend our lives preparing for events. If we are going on a trip we make plans. We get airline tickets, we buy clothes, and we book hotels. If we are having a baby we get ready .We get cribs and strollers and diapers .We plan for Christmas months in advance. We buy a tree and decorate to be ready. We spend our life planning for everything important …but love. Love is one of the most important things and yet we never get ready for it.

Getting ready for love means working on yourself. It takes time and isn't easy. It means digging deep within yourself to see what you really want. It takes being in a place where you see your worth and know what you truly deserve. It involves finding the things that bring you joy and happiness. Once you find these things you need to cultivate them. You need to walk away from anything that enters into your bubble of happiness. It means turning off the television and screens. Instead spend time outdoors looking up at the stars, walking a beach, hiking a mountain or a quiet walk in the woods.

Preparing for love can take months or years. It is the single most important thing to do for yourself. Work on your inside until you are a hurricane of optimism and joy.

The minute you are in that space, people will notice it. You will be ready. Once you are in this space, open the door with arms outstretched, and you will be amazed at what life gives you.

Chapter 1

Tuesday started out its ordinary way with my usual routine of getting ready for work. Brushing my teeth and looking in the mirror, I realized I had just turned 60. I had a fabulous life. I had a dream job selling manufactured homes and making really great money.

My network of girl friends, known as the tribe, met a few times a week for wine on Wednesdays and any other occasion we could dream up. I'd been blessed with a great son who's successful in real estate. Most importantly, I lived at the beach in a charming little fishing village called Murrells Inlet. But something wasn't right in my life. What was I missing?

All at once, a feeling of loneliness swept over me. But I wasn't lonely for dates as I had dated a lot. A real connection with someone was what I longed for in my life. I wanted a soul mate, someone to finish the journey with me. This feeling kept nagging at me throughout my busy day. I spent the day showing houses and wrote two contracts, but I still had that strange feeling of emptiness.

After work, I drove to the beach and walked for about an hour. I'm very strange, as I only enjoyed the beach after most people had left for the day. Most of my thinking occurred at the beach, either at sunrise or sunset. I loved the solitude and quiet the beach offered. On this particular beach walk, I made a decision to try a dating site, Plenty of Fish, as this feeling wasn't going away. I had tried the site a few times, mainly out of curiosity, rather than to actually find someone.

After getting home, I poured a glass of wine, put on some relaxing Diana Krall music, and began reading profiles. However, I didn't just skim the words this time. I wanted to understand what each person was trying to convey through his profile. The usual profiles were about sports, working out, movies, and hobbies. It was easy to spot people who were not a match for me, but there were so many men and all so different. Scrolling through the endless profiles was like shopping in a candy store. This time, though, I knew I was ready. My checklist of important characteristics and qualities stood ready to go and settling for anyone less than the best didn't enter the picture.

Would I be able to find that someone? My bar was set really high. They say you get what you expect; well, I expected quite the guy.

Chapter 2

I scrolled through profiles until I saw a face which made me look twice. I clicked on his profile and noticed a great looking guy. But his profile said widower, so I hesitated to reach out. Looking through his profile, I saw various photos and loved one picture showing his facial hair and shades. That look definitely attracted me.

Then, one particular picture stopped me from scrolling. I couldn't help but notice this man's beautiful cornflower blue eyes, but a certain sadness also reflected in them. While reading his bio, something tugged at me. I liked what he was about, and he sounded thoughtful and kind. This guy's profile showed shots of him doing the usual things, such as displaying family and animal photos. The best part about his profile? He lived in the next town over from me. Thinking I had nothing to lose, I decided to send him a message. His screen name was Stone. I was trying to figure out just what to say. I had just gotten on this site and hadn't messaged anyone. I started typing a message and kept deleting it as it sounded horrible. I wasn't sure how I wanted to come across. Finally, after about twenty attempts for the perfect message, I sent one. I didn't get all creative and just typed, "Very nice profile and you live close". I looked at the time, and since it was only 9:30, I thought he'd surely reply. At midnight, I fell asleep thinking about his intriguing face.

Chapter 3

The next morning, I put a lot of effort into getting ready for work. It was wine Wednesday and tribe night. On Wednesdays, we all gathered at one of the great restaurants on the Marsh Walk to share a great meal and to catch up. My tribe, a crazy and unique group of women, proved very different from one other. We never judged each other and rarely questioned how we all found each other even though our tribe each came from a different state.

A gorgeous day unfolded as I arrived at work that Wednesday morning. Ready to start my day, I sat down at my desk and grabbed my ever present cup of coffee. Just then, I heard my phone ding and opened my Plenty of Fish app to see that Stone had replied.

Sweetly he responded, "What a nice face to wake up to. I'm sorry I didn't respond last night but spent the day on the beach and went to bed pretty early. I'm on vacation in the area and would love to meet you for a drink tonight if possible."

That dispelled my theory that he must have had another date since he didn't respond last night. Vacation. Tribe night. Oh no, don't tell me he's a vacationer! No one wants to just meet a golfer on vacation!

I replied, "Oh gosh, tonight I get together with all my girl friends for drinks. We meet for happy hour, but we're usually done around eight o'clock."

"I could meet you after if that would be okay."

"Yeah, that would be great. We're meeting at Bovines at 7 o'clock."

"I hate texting through this Plenty of Fish app," said Stone. "Would it be okay if I send you my number and we can text instead of having to open the app?"

"Yes, that certainly would be easier as I'm at work, and it would be better for me as well."

So, he sent me his number and we began texting a few times during the day.

Stone texted, "So are you working hard and having a good day?"

"It sure seems to be getting better with each funny text you send," I replied.

Curiosity and excitement consumed me as I anticipated that evening. Of course, my work day got nuts. I ended up selling a house and never made it to Bovines in the inlet until after seven-thirty. So much for getting changed and looking great for the first time we were to meet

I arrived at Bovines, and looking through the side door, I could see all of the tribe had settled in and were having fun. I visited for a few minutes and looked across the bar. There, all by himself, sat Stone - tan, cute, and a golfer type. He glanced up at me, smirked, and then looked down at his phone. Gosh he's cute, I thought to myself as I walked over to talk to him.

I came up beside him and said, "Hey there, I'm Maddie. It's so nice to meet you."

"And I'm Stone. Well, you're quite the surprise. You're not the corporate realtor type."

I laughed and said, "Well, that's a good thing then."

"You certainly have the group of ladies over there," Stone commented. "Where did you all meet?"

"Some I've sold homes, a few I've met through mutual friends, some do nails, one or two own shops, and one is an accountant. We've all just become like family and spend a lot of time together."

Stone said, "I told the bartender I was meeting a girl from the tribe. I asked if he knew you, and he said you all had nicknames. I showed him your picture and asked him if I should run or stay? He said, 'Oh, that's Blondie. You should stay. She's the tribe leader and a good one.'"

"Oh that's too funny. Should you run? That should be a definite no."

We talked for a few more minutes and what was to be a quick hello turned into a fifteen minute conversation. This man intrigued and completely melted me with his North Carolina accent, his smile and cute expressions. I finally invited him over to meet my girls, who I'd all but forgotten. When Stone turned on the barstool, I saw he had a prosthetic leg, and that totally threw me off guard.

"Oh, wow! What happened to you?"

"Let's just say there's one less great white out in the ocean."

"Oh, that's just awful. I'm so sorry."

With a wink, Stone replied, "Are you really that blonde? No, actually I was involved in a lawnmower accident at age five. My neighbor's son was mowing the grass, and my buddy and I were playing on the hill. He backed up and didn't see my foot. The doctors were unable to save my foot, but I'm lucky to have full use of my leg. The accident happened so long ago."

Stunned, I didn't know what to say. He and I headed over to see my friends. I could tell the girls thought he was funny and nice. I watched him interact with them; his ease with everyone surprised me. This guy certainly caught my attention.

After the girls left, we went inside for a drink. Then

we took a walk on the beautiful, romantic marsh walk. Stone and I had so much to say to one another, and I wanted to know everything about him.

Stone lived in Asheville, North Carolina. It turned out that the dating app follows where you are, so that is why it showed he lived near me. We discovered that he and I had both moved various times. I was married to a corporate executive, and Stone had a career with Marriott. We bonded over hotels, as he ran them, and I'd previously worked in a few. We shared stories about our crazy lives. Showing each other pictures of our homes, we laughed as they looked almost identical.

Keeping an open mind, I thought, wow, what an interesting, genuine, sweet man. We had both recently set up accounts on Plenty of Fish. I'd asked the universe for this kind of guy. The chances of finding someone like Stone was like finding a needle in a haystack. His family of thirty-nine planned on arriving in one night, and if he hadn't checked his app, we would never have met. *Fate had a hand in this!*

The still water next to the Marsh Walk reflected a full moon and a sky full of stars. But this magical moment unfortunately vanished all too quickly. All of the restaurants were closing. The time had flown by.

Stone asked, "Do you know what time it is?"

"It's probably about eleven."

"No! It's almost one in the morning!"

We both started laughing. He walked me to my car and gave me a kiss on the cheek. I had a great feeling about him. When I got home, my phone went off with a text. I smiled realizing it was from this adorable guy.

Stone said, "I have to say I had a great time tonight. I can't believe we stayed out so late. I would like to see you on Friday since my two daughters won't be in till Saturday. The rest of my family will be here, but I would like to see you again."

"I think we can make that happen," I answered. "We can meet at Wahoos at around eight-thirty. It'll be very crowded since a great band will be playing."

He texted, "Is it Friday yet? Get some sleep. We'll talk soon."

Many thoughts swirled through my head. Asheville… five and a half hours from here, a huge family, two grown daughters, and a widower. But somehow, despite all these situations, none of them seemed like an issue.

Chapter 4

Friday night, we decided to start with a drink at Wahoos. His family had arrived, with the exception of his children, who'd arrive later. Wahoos always proved to be a fun place and usually had the best bands.

I took excruciating pains to look fabulous for Stone. Arriving home early from work, I got tanned, dressed in a great off the shoulder top, tight ripped jeans, and killer shoes.

Stone texted, "I'll find you at the bar."

My guy greeted me with a huge smile, ordered drinks, grabbed my hand in his, and we never looked back. For the next three hours, Stone and I held hands; I couldn't get enough of this amazing man.

Finally, the beautiful inlet showed signs of closing, so I called an Uber. Stone had tried to get an Uber, as well, but the app didn't seem to be working on his phone. I suggested we share one, which was so unlike me. First, the Uber driver took me home. As a cautious person, this felt weird to me. I wasn't sure I wanted Stone to know exactly where I lived just yet. However, because I had such a good feeling about him, my apprehension soon dissolved.

Pulling up at my condo, the Uber driver commented, "Are you going to walk her to the door? If not, I sure will!" What a hilarious moment!

So, Stone proceeded to walk me to my stairwell and planted a really nice kiss on my mouth. I could have flown up my steps. What was it about this guy?

Right away he texted, "We'll figure out a day next week to have lunch since my family will all be in town."

I knew his huge family vacation was underway and would be held at Litchfield by the Sea. Stone had five brothers and sisters, their kids, his two daughters, and his mom. The vacation setting consisted of four beach houses, golf carts, golf tee times, and every night a family dinner. I loved his wholesomeness and that he was so family oriented. This checked another box on my list.

Tuesday we met at my office and planned to go to lunch. I was really nervous as I rarely brought dates to my office. When he walked in, I thought, oh my God, he looks great. A hot mess described me. I showed him my pretty front office and my board with all the homes I'd recently sold. I think he was pretty impressed.

Stone and I went to J Peters and ordered two huge salads but barely ate a lettuce leaf. We held hands, talked, and stared at each other, feeling seventeen again. At one point, he excused himself to visit the men's room.

I texted, "Omg, I'm having such a fun time."

Before leaving the restaurant, I went to the ladies' room, and he texted me , "You're amazing."

After lunch, my new guy brought me back to my office. All I wanted to do was freeze time and didn't want to get out of that car. We kissed in the parking lot, and I thought he's pretty damn nice.

Later in the afternoon, he texted, "I hope we'll see each other before the week is over." I said a silent prayer that we surely would make that happen!

Chapter 5

The next few days Stone and I texted often. He described his crazy vacation and how exhausting it was lying on the beach all day. The pictures he sent were the tents and a yeti full of cold Bud Lights. It didn't seem like tough days to me, as I was toiling away at work.

He knew I was leaving for a girls trip to Savannah on Saturday. I knew he was leaving the beach to go back to Asheville on Sunday morning. We both had discussed this a few times. We were trying to come up with a plan to see each other before I left.

Stone texted, "Can we meet for coffee before you leave?"

"I would love that, but the girls are leaving at ten a.m."

"We can meet at Starbucks in Litchfield by the Sea around seven," he answered.

"Seven as in the morning?"

"Yes, so we can have coffee, and I can take you on a golf cart ride around Litchfield by the Sea. I want to show it to you."

"Okay. That would be great...early, but great!"

I awoke at zero dark thirty to get showered and to do my hair and makeup. However, as I walked out the door, the weather had changed to pouring rain. I drove to Starbucks and ran through a "monsoon" to get inside. Swinging open the door, I saw Stone walking toward me. Dressed in a black t-shirt, khakis, and with his hair all combed, I thought again how much I really liked this guy. We ordered coffee and held hands as we sat on the couch in front of the fireplace. But despite staying there for three hours, our time together seemed to end all too quickly, and we said our goodbyes again. Before leaving, we took a picture of us, both in black t-shirts and huge smiles. We ran to our cars in a downpour, grabbed a quick kiss, and each drove our separate ways. Pumped and excited, I knew this was going to be something epic.

On the way to Savannah, I drove my girl friends insane talking about Stone. Our lengthy conversations discussed dating at this age, starting over with someone new, and having sex with that person. I also had concerns about his prosthetic leg. But the big questions discussed the potential problems of long distance relationships and how to sustain them over time.

The weekend was a blast with my best girlies. We shopped, explored the beautiful city, did lots of day drinking, and had some fabulous dinners. In the background of this fun weekend, I thought about this man with this incredibly deep sexy accent.

Stone and I talked a bit during my visit to Savannah while he drove back home. His driving out of my state felt strange to me, and I already missed him. But we'd decided to talk after the weekend, and Sunday night couldn't get here fast enough.

Chapter 6

Sunday night I couldn't contain myself. I took a shower, poured a glass of wine and waited for Stone to call. The minute I heard that deep voice with that damned accent my heart started racing. We laughed and talked about his family vacation and all about my crazy trip to Savannah. It was as if we just picked up from where we'd left off. There were no awkward silences. We both wanted to know all about each other, since we'd spent about 50 years in a different lifetime.

During the course of our conversations, we discovered our families, kids, and places where we'd each lived were very similar. We both enjoyed all the moves to different states. Our kids were around the same age. I'd raised a son, and he'd raised two daughters. We discussed my divorce and about the loss of his wife. We filled in the gaps about each other. Our talk led to discussion about life in the Carolinas. Stone spoke about his love of the mountains; I chatted about my love of the beach.

Our conversations continued to last until the

wee hours of the morning, and we discovered many similarities in our personalities as well.

I worked the next morning with very little sleep, and yet I never felt more alive. The day flew, and all I could think about was talking to this beautiful man. For the next three and a half weeks, my days consisted of work with very little sleep, cute texts throughout the day, and nightly phone calls. Finally, we decided I would go visit Stone.

He'd simply stated, "I want you to see my world."

Those words hit me like a ton of bricks. This incredible man wanted to show me the place where he'd grown up in Asheville, North Carolina. I couldn't wait to see this world of mountains, streams, and waterfalls.

The big day finally arrived. My son and best girl friends knew my plans and also Stone's address. I was to drive to Asheville on Thursday morning and back to Murrells Inlet, South Carolina on Sunday. But absolutely horrible with directions, I couldn't even begin to tell you how nervous I was about the drive. The ride was five and a half hours away, and I'd never even been past Columbia. I hashed and rehashed this trip with my two girlfriends. I was unsure what to wear the day of the trip and what to pack. I also worried about where I would sleep. I was terrified of the, "*what ifs,*" but also excited. My heart was already invested in this guy, and that worried me greatly. I grabbed my suitcase and a large coffee and locked my door.

I wanted to see where this journey would lead. On the ride, I listened to every love song imaginable. I always trusted my gut and just felt in my spirit that everything would be great.

Stone called a few times to check my progress. Each time I just smiled down at the phone.

He said, "Hey Baby are you doing okay? Make sure you have gas and snacks and keep your phone charged."

"Yes dad," I laughed. "I stopped and got gas before I left . I have a huge coffee and tons of snacks. I feel like I'm on a field trip."

"Take your time and be careful. I don't want anything happening to you."

"You're so sweet. I'll text you when I get closer."

Eventually, I got to Spartanburg and called him. "I see mountains!"

Stone laughed and said, "Baby, you're like an hour from me, and just so you know, I live *on* the mountain."

Seeing those mountains and hearing his voice at that exact moment was perfect. I felt everything had led me to you.

I hadn't seen Stone since July, and it was now the second week of August. Thoughts of doubt rushed through my head. Would he still like me? And would I still like him? Was I making a mistake? Is this too far a distance? Is this too good to be true?

At 3:30, I drove up a hill and then pulled up to his charming, tan ranch house with black shutters and pretty front yard. My heart pounded, and suddenly, I hated the black t-shirt dress I had on. Then, I spotted Stone coming down the walkway wearing a huge smile and holding the cutest little dog named Honey. We both sized each other up, and I thought, here goes. Walking into his home felt absolutely perfect.

We embraced, and he gave me a quick kiss on the cheek. "Welcome to my world, Maddie. I thought you'd never get here."

"Well, it was a pretty long ride, and of course, I made some stops. I'm so excited to be here and to see everything you've told me about. So, show me your house."

We started to tour his house but didn't get far. As I stood in his living room and faced a wall of massive windows, the view of the spectacular mountains astonished me. A gorgeous stone fireplace took up half the wall of the beautiful living room.

I said, "Oh my God, this is simply stunning."

"So my girl approves of the mountain view?"

"Are you kidding me? I feel like I'm in the *Sound of Music*."

We went out to the patio, and the mountains took my breath away. I knew from all of our conversations how much he loved music. When I went back into the house, Neil Young's "Harvest Moon" played in the background. That song will always be the one which reminds me of this magical place.

My sweet man said, "There are three bedrooms. You can stay wherever you choose. There's no pressure, but I hope you'll choose mine."

We opened up a bottle of wine, and the evening was on!

Chapter 7

I knew you were nervous as well. Even though we knew so much about each other, we didn't know one another physically. How would this play out? I looked at your face and loved it. We needed to be comfortable in order to have a great time. The wine and that amazing music made it easy to see just what we had found in each other. I also knew the pent up crazy passion needed to be released and no doubt the physical would be great.

Stone said, "I can't believe you are really here, baby. I feel like we know each other from our conversations every night for the last six weeks."

"I haven't felt like this in such a long time, Stone. Maybe we should see how the rest of this is going to work out."

"Are you saying what I'm thinking?" he asked.

I took his hand in mine. "This little vixen is saying exactly that."

We proceeded down to the bedroom with our glasses

of wine. Our lovemaking resembled a movie scene with a hallway littered with clothes. Our mouths acted like they had never been kissed. I never wanted anything more, needed to feel you, needed to kiss you and make love to you. This was our very first time. Everything was perfect, not textbook perfect. It was exactly the way it should be.

Afterwards, we lay there for a moment. Then, looking into his eyes, I couldn't help but laugh. "What the hell just happened?"

He sighed deeply and pulled me close. "I have no idea, baby. Wow."_

We both knew this was pretty damned good between us.

Our situation was so different. We'd met on-line in another state, only dated four times, shared a few kisses, and did a lot of hand holding. There was no first base, no second base. This was what set us apart. In six weeks, we'd fallen in love with our hearts and heads. It was the absolute best way to fall. Our bodies came second. I fell in love with Stone before I set foot in Asheville. I knew the moment I looked at him the very first time that he was the one I'd been waiting for.

After finishing our wine, Stone showed me around his town. What spectacular beauty! The best parts, though, were sitting in his jeep with his hand in mine, listening to great tunes on the radio, and feeling the sunshine pouring through the windows. I just wanted to savor every second. Gazing at this incredible man, I thought, oh my God, how can this be so real and so good?

Chapter 8

The beauty of Asheville amazed me, and to say I was in awe was an understatement. We went to Buzzards Rock, a local spot of high elevation. The rock was covered with graffiti, but when one sat way up on it, an incredible view presented itself. Stone and I sat and talked, and I remember thinking, wow, this is really different. I absolutely adored the loveliness of this stunning location. We took a picture with the gorgeous scenery as a backdrop, and later Stone made that his profile picture. Stop my heart.

Later in the day, we drove to and explored the Blue Ridge Parkway. I think my jaw hit the ground with each magnificent area I viewed. Stone saved one very special place for last, and yes, that pretty much sealed the deal.

At last, we left the Blue Ridge Parkway and headed to the Grove Park Inn. Driving up to the entrance, I had no words to describe this impressive building. Made of stone, the inn's charming red roof draped almost like a mushroom. Massive wooden doors and rocking chairs along the stone porch greeted us. Stone took my hand, and when we entered the lobby, the room's architecture completely blew me away. I'd never seen such incredibly high ceilings, beams, and a room flanked by the most enormous fireplaces. A person could actually stand inside them, and one fireplace even had an elevator inside! Adding to the ambiance, the lobby was also comfortably decorated with gorgeous rocking chairs, other sumptuous furniture, and lovely local art of mountain scenery.

Stone and I ordered a glass of wine, and just when I didn't think it could get any better, we walked out the door to what's known as the Sunset Terrace. By far, the terrace had to be the prettiest, most magical place I'd ever experienced. Sitting at a tiny table on the fabulous stone steps with a glass of wine, Stone and I viewed the picturesque Blue Ridge Mountains at sunset.

"Thank you for bringing me here, Stone. I love that you want to share all this world with me."

"I knew this place would blow you away, Maddie. I saved coming here for last. This is what they call a million dollar view."

" I can certainly see why. It's stunning and so surreal."

"It's been said whoever brings you here, you'll eventually fall in love," Stone said softly.

I rolled my eyes and laughed. "You just made that up."

"Maybe, but I hear it's true."

"You were looking at the time on your phone, so we would be in this spot. You wanted me to be on the sunset terrace as the big ball of sun set."

He replied, "Yes, what better way to see sunset in the mountains than at Grove Park Inn."

We were both caught up in this beautiful moment and knew pretty powerful stuff was happening. This sweet man planned our visit perfectly so I could see my first sunset in Asheville. This is the stuff of fairytales.

After that fabulous experience, Stone and I drove back to his house to get ready for dinner. I asked, "Where are you taking me for dinner?"

"I thought we'd go to a place called Avenue M. It's a local spot and you'll love the food. They have steak medallions which are a fan favorite."

"I don't know, Stone, but you're certainly knocking it out of the park. Steak and mashed potatoes are my weakness. You seem to be my weakness, too."

"Is that a fact, Blondie? I like the sound of that."

That made me laugh. "Who are you? I have had such a great time already. I love that you planned all of this."

Avenue M proved to be an adorable place with a great vibe. We enjoyed our time there, and Stone introduced me to the owners. I loved being near a local neighborhood restaurant.

During what proved to be another fabulous date, I learned a lot about his family. So I asked, "Your family really all live close by?"

"I have three sisters and one brother. One brother died a few years ago, one of my sisters lives in Atlanta, but everyone else lives here. My mother lives here as well. We're all best friends. We talk on the phone often and see each other pretty much every day, and also live about two miles from each other. This weekend you'll probably meet most of them."

A feeling of trepidation swept over me. "What? I'm going to meet most of your family? I'm not sure I'm ready for all of that."

But Stone's soothing voice reassured me. "They'll love you, Maddie. Trust me, baby. You'll see."

Earlier in the day, we stopped at the Grove Park Gallery. It's a beautiful shop filled with pottery and jewelry from local artists. Suddenly, this man came up behind me and said, "You must be the beach girl." I looked at his face and knew immediately this must be his brother. He was so friendly and couldn't have been nicer.

His comment made me break into laughter. "How can you tell I'm the beach girl? The fact that I'm in flip flops? Maybe because you heard everything about me from your brother? I'm sure he told you nothing but all good things."

"Well, he's been talking about you quite a bit. I was looking forward to meeting the girl who seems to be putting a smile on his face."

From that very first day, Stone's brother and I connected. He made me feel very welcome. I could also see the close bond between these two brothers.

I experienced such a great first day in Asheville, and I still had two more days with this fabulous guy!

Chapter 9

Day two, I walked out of the shower to the smell of pancakes, bacon and coffee. Great music from the '80s drifted throughout the house. Then, a song from *Saturday Night Fever* came on. I laughed and asked myself, who was this adorable man who made me breakfast, loved music, and whose smile stunned me. I just had to give him a big hug and a kiss right on his beautiful mouth.

"Where are you taking your girl today?"

"I'm taking you to a famous brewery called Sierra Nevada. It's a very cool place. I'm not a big fan of IPA beers, but the grounds are gorgeous. It's located on the French Broad River, and I think my girl will love it." He reached over and embraced me lovingly along with a great big kiss.

"I've heard of it, and I'm not sure I'd like IPA beers either since I've never had one. I may not like the beers, but I sure do like you. The sun is out, it's a gorgeous day, and I'm with you."

29

On our way to the Sierra Nevada Brewery, Stone's phone rang. It was his mother. "I'm having lunch with the girls later this afternoon," she explained. "But right now, I'm having trouble keeping the patio umbrella up. Can you stop by?"

"Well Mom, I'm just heading out to Sierra Nevada with Maddie."

He looked at me smirking and said, "Trust me there's nothing wrong with the umbrella. She just wants to meet the beach girl."

"You said she lives close by. Let's run over for a minute, and you can take a look at it."

We pulled up to a huge brick ranch home with a carport and mother-in-law suite. I assumed Stone would just run in, and I'd sit in the car and wait. But that certainly wasn't going to happen because he had other plans.

"You really need to come inside. My mother would think it was rude of me to leave you out here."

I looked into his caring eyes and smiled at him. "Okay, I guess I'm going inside."

I thought, I'm sixty years old and meeting someone's mom for the first time. I hadn't done that in a very, very long time. Stone absolutely adored his mother, and she was his rock. So, I walked into her home and immediately felt so comfortable. Childhood pictures graced the walls, and I realized this was his childhood home. His mom came over to greet me, and I liked her the minute we met. A little dynamo, this lady radiated energy. She dressed to the nines and wore matching pants, a pretty top, and great flat shoes.

Mrs. Stone radiated Southern grace and charm. Graciously, she smiled and took my hand in hers. "Well it's certainly nice to meet you, Maddie. I've been hearing all about the beach girl. I have to say, though, you aren't what I expected. I thought you were a girl, but you are a woman."

I smiled realizing she probably thought I was about 35 years old covered in tattoos. Getting acquainted, I proceeded to tell her a little bit about myself. I could tell she loved the fact that I was educated and a former elementary teacher and knew she loved that I now worked selling manufactured homes.

While Stone fixed the umbrella on her deck, his mother and I continued to chat. I noticed a book she had been reading on her table. "Oh, so you're a reader, too? I've read many books by that same author. I love any beach stories."

She replied. "I always have a book started. I enjoy losing myself in them. My problem is I always forget if I had read it before."

We both laughed after that comment. "I always forget, too. I read so much. I will start a book and read a few pages and realize I know the story. You and I agree there's nothing like curling up with a blanket and a new book."

We also talked about how both of us loved being at the beach in South Carolina. She told me how their family had been going to Litchfield by the Sea for over twenty-five years. She'd walk the beach every morning and read in the afternoon. I realized I did the very same thing. I kept thinking how strange to have all of this unfold.

I couldn't believe I was sitting in Stone's childhood home sharing iced tea and stories with his sweet mom. I loved seeing him around her. She certainly raised an incredible son. I loved spending time with this lovely lady. Stone seemed so happy that she and I got along so well. As we were leaving, she invited us to church on Saturday night and also invited us for supper. I left her home feeling that she was a huge part of this Asheville life.

Stone and I skipped the brewery and just did lunch, made a few stops in the downtown area, and then we visited some amazing rooftop bars. Everywhere we went, this wonderful man and I held hands and stole a few kisses along the way. I had fallen for this guy!

Unexpectedly, his sister called and invited us to a wine bar that night. We drove to her home, which I absolutely loved. Later, we took an Uber downtown. She and I got along great and had such a fun time listening to music and getting to know one another. Finally, we left to return to her house. I got out of the Uber to give her a hug and to say how much fun I'd had. Stone closed the Uber door, and it drove away. I assumed we were taking the Uber back to Stone's house, so I didn't really pay attention.

Then it hit me. Oh my God! The Uber had driven away with my purse in the back seat! But not only had my purse vanished with the Uber, but everything I owned was inside that purse, including my phone, wallet, keys, and glasses. I suddenly realized I'd have to depend on Stone for everything. We tried calling Uber, left tons of messages, and went home figuring we'd hear something in the morning. I was surprised I wasn't out of my mind with worry. Relying on Stone so much felt strange, yet I knew I was in great hands. I had a sense of peace and calm around this man. I had faith all would turn out okay and that tomorrow we'd get a call from Uber.

Chapter 10

On Saturday, we tried to reach Uber but still got no response. We tried to keep our mind off the situation by deciding to go downtown for lunch.

Stone asked, "Are you worried we won't get a call, Maddie?"

"Yes, it is very concerning since I have to go home on Sunday and work on Monday. I'm very surprised we haven't heard anything yet. But I'm sure by dinnertime we'll get a call. If we don't, then we'll figure something out."

Anxiety swept over me, and I felt sure Stone probably thought, oh my God, what am I going to do with her? She has no way to get home, no license, and no phone. But actually, Stone didn't seem to be that worried.

His kind words reassured me. "Maddie, baby, don't you worry about anything. Everything's going to be okay. You'll see. It's just a matter of time, and we'll soon hear from Uber.

In the middle of lunch, Stone's best friend called, and he explained what had happened. He asked to speak with me. I took the phone and his friend said, "I know we have not met. I want to let you know you're with one of the best families in Asheville. You have no idea how wonderful and loved they are in this town. You have nothing to worry about. They'll rent a car for you, fly you home, and do whatever it takes. Please relax, Everything will be just fine."

We stuck with the plan of going to church with Stone's family and then to have dinner at his mom's house. I'd packed a dress and was sure Stone's mom loved that I dressed for church. I loved that the family all sat together. Before mass started his mom reached over to me saying, "Don't worry about your purse. We'll say a prayer to St. Anthony, and everything will work out," she said, as she squeezed my hand,

Her caring words instantly made me feel better. "Aw, thank you, Mrs. Stone. I hope you're right."

I looked at this beautiful woman and saw her faith, and again I felt reassured. A wonderful feeling came over me as I sat in this beautiful church with Stone's family, their missals opened and singing every word. I hadn't been to church with anyone in over twenty years. Within that moment, I honestly didn't care about anything else.

I could have stayed there with this family and been very happy. I didn't worry about my job and all the missed phone calls. My son and my two best friends knew what had happened with Stone. I felt so safe with this man. I kept sneaking looks at him singing and knowing every word. My hand was on the church pew, and he locked pinkies with me. Looking around this church, I thought, I want him, and I want this world of his.

My faith was different from Stone's. After my divorce, I felt a little lost. One day, I found myself walking into St. Michaels church, and I lit a candle. I have not missed a week lighting a candle in almost fifteen years! I spend about twenty minutes being grateful for everything I've been given. I look at the stained glass and the sunshine pouring through the quiet church. It's on this spot that I dug deep to find me again. I learned to take each day as a gift. The last few months, I have prayed to find a partner, a friend, a lover, and someone who sees life as I do. I wanted a positive thinking man, full of joy, and someone who appreciated all the importance in life. Then, you miraculously arrived.

Chapter 11

During the church service, the ushers passed the basket, and of course, I had no money. I whispered in his ear, "Can I have some money to put in the basket?"

Stone smirked and rolled his eyes. "Wow, sure sucks to be you." He then handed me a five dollar bill, looked at me, and winked.

I'd wanted to buy a bottle of wine and a dessert to take to his mom's house for dinner, but with no money, that was impossible, of course. So, Stone had to spend money on those items, too.

The family gathering proved to be such a treat. Stone's sweet mother had bought all the fixings for a heavenly Southern after church dinner: chicken, biscuits, mashed potatoes, gravy, and coleslaw.

Stone's cousin arrived and heard my unfortunate story about my lost items. As it turned out, his cousin's friend was a big wig for Uber, and she kindly placed a call to him. He told her about a special number to call which Stone so sweetly did for me.

His beautiful mom grabbed my hand. "It will all work out."

The funny thing was, I didn't worry at that moment. I glanced around at this man and his beautiful family and just wanted to stay right there. I'd never met such a close-knit family as this one.

During the course of our dinner, Stone's phone rang. Everyone got silent. The call came from the Uber driver from the previous night. He had my purse in his trunk all night but had his phone turned off and had slept all day.

The driver met us at the grocery store around the corner. I jumped out of the jeep and hugged him and gave him a large tip. My purse was intact and not a thing was missing. All was right with my world!

We went back to finish dinner, and Stone's mom flashed us a huge smile. Because of her devout faith, this kind lady never worried. Dinner ended way too quickly, but I had this last night to spend with Stone.

Chapter 12

Sunday morning unfolded as a beautiful sunny day. Stone fixed breakfast and then made a yeti of coffee for my ride home. I didn't want to leave. The weekend proved beyond magical, even with a lost purse. The views, the music, the meals, the hand-holding and kisses, and the looks we shared were incredible. Meeting the family and seeing Stone around them made me fall even more for him. I have lived enough of life to know this was genuine. This man was the piece of my puzzle, so open, honest, and real.

As we packed the car, I sat in the driver's seat with the door open, and the strangest thing happened. Honey jumped up into my lap and started licking my face nonstop. I was told that the dog never goes in anyone's car. Stone looked stunned.

"Come here, Honey. She needs to go home. Come on girl, you need to come here."

"Oh wow. This is so strange, Stone. The more you call her, the more she licks my face. I'm not sure what to do."

He tried taking her off my lap, but she wouldn't budge. Finally, he opened the passenger door and literally pulled her off me.

"I'm not sure why she did that. How very strange. I think she thought you were my deceased wife, and she doesn't want you to leave. I'm not sure I want you to leave either, Maddie."

"Wow, that was so eerie," I said. "Your beautiful dog has great taste. I had the absolute best time here, and I hate to leave you, too, Stone."

I put the car in reverse and drove down the mountain in tears. All I wanted to do was to turn around and run back to the little gem on the hill.

The ride went quickly as I replayed the magical weekend over and over again in my mind. I continued to marvel how this man had made everything so completely special. When Stone and I were together, I felt so at home because he was so kind, thoughtful, and easy to be with. Lying next to him in bed, I silently prayed, how did I get so damned lucky? I truly loved him with everything within my being. I thought about Honey and that eerie experience. He called me a few times on my drive home, and I believed in my heart this guy was the one for me. The checklist was pretty much hit, and this first weekend sealed our relationship for me. Stone completed the whole package with his faith and tenderness. But what next, though?

Chapter 13

The pattern was pretty set. A week of phone calls and texts turned each other's world upside down. Next week he'd visit my world. However, I felt somewhat unsure about his visit as I have a condo on the third floor with no elevator and no place to grill. I refer to my stairs as either the stairway to heaven or the highway to hell. Once inside, my place was bright, open, and airy. The screen porch faces the second hole of a golf course.

Stone arrived, and bam! We were on; the chemistry was so good between us. Stone seemed to like my place, and walking out onto the porch, he noticed the golf course. "You actually live on a golf course. What nine is this and which hole?"

"I know you love golf, and I thought you'd love playing this course. It's the front nine and my view is the second hole. If you're lucky, when the course closes, you can practice on that hole. You can do sand shots out of the bunker, chipping to the green and practice putting."

He asked, "Do they have a driving range? And do they have a practice putting green?"

"This golf course has it all. Their pro shop is cute. There's a little grill room and a great back porch overlooking the eighteenth hole. And they even have ice cold beers and quite a few gators."

This would be another weekend of firsts…first time in my bed, first time golfing together, and first time meeting my son. I'd made a lot of loose plans and most meals would be out. What a blast we'd have.

"So, my beach girl, what have you planned for us to do?"

"Well, I hope you aren't tired, because I've got a bunch of things planned."

The weekend was spent doing all sorts of fun things. We played golf at Blackmoor and had lunch at the beautiful Caledonia. Walking around the marsh walk was so much fun, and we stopped for a drink at one of the amazing restaurants. I showed Stone where I worked and drove to see Garden City Beach and Surf Side Beach. We explored all the beauty of Murrells Inlet. In the evening we dined at gorgeous restaurants, notably Frank's and Bistro 217. Each night, we spent romantic evenings on the porch with candles, pretty music, and wine. I loved seeing Stone in my home; having him there with me just felt right. Lovemaking was off the charts as our bodies were so in tune. It seemed as though we were always in constant arousal. Could this really be happening? How could everything be so damned hot?

Chapter 14

The weekend at my house proved fabulous, but one episode happened which especially bonded Stone and me closer than ever.

We had finished golfing and were getting ready to go out for dinner. I was in the bathroom putting on mascara, and Stone walked into my bedroom. He said he wanted to show me something.

I thought maybe he wanted to show me a text or something on his phone. Then, I looked at his face. "What's wrong baby? Are you okay?"

Stone said, "This could be a deal breaker…if you aren't sure you can handle it."

Realizing he'd taken off his prosthetic, Stone stood there more vulnerable than I ever imagined. I looked into his eyes and thought this defining moment could change everything. My incredible man had suffered such a tragic accident at age five.

Then, I got on my knees and kissed where his foot was missing. I said gently, "Not a deal breaker at all."

We both had tears in our eyes, and I knew at that moment, more than ever, a solid bond had formed.

Most people would not have handled the loss of a foot the way Stone had. Blessed to have a family who treated him just like everyone else, his amazing mother made him her center. As a child, he'd climbed trees, played sports, rode bikes, and had the same opportunities to do everything his siblings enjoyed. He wrestled all through high school and became captain of the wrestling team. This incredible mom even went to the board to have the laws changed so that Stone could wrestle.

Mrs. Stone told me about the time when her son got his very first job at a restaurant. After he'd finished filling out the application, she'd looked it over. She read a question which asked if there was any physical reason or any disability that could hinder him from doing the job. Stone answered no. That said it all. He never felt different at all. Through his family's love and support, Stone became a confident successful man.

After the accident, this five year old child spent four months in a hospital and had four surgeries. His beautiful mom sat by his side all day even though there were five siblings at home. A very special bond had developed between them. Imagine being in a hospital where no one could visit you for four months. On Sundays, the family pulled up in their wooden station wagon, and his brother and sisters would wave and cheer out to him. Talk about an incredible family!

During our first meeting, Mrs. Stone had confided in me that her son's lawnmower accident was the worst day of her life. But he called it his godsend. Losing his foot in the accident made him more aware, at a young age, of people's differences. He never, ever showed anger, negativity, or used the accident to his advantage. Pity parties never entered into the picture, either.

Chapter 15

The loss of Stone's wife was tragic and painful. I'd heard so many stories about her, I felt I knew her. We shared so many things in common. We both loved candles, cards, and stationery. Neither of us had a sense of direction.

I'd found out that she didn't want Stone to be alone, and because of this, she allowed him to heal. I knew she made him incredibly happy, and I could only hope to make him happy as well...but happy in another way. Stone's a different man now; life and time have changed him. All I could promise was to show him love the best way I knew how.

The weeks flew by, and long distance is good. Anticipation adds to the coming excitement. Stone and I discussed Columbia, South Carolina as our next meeting place, since it's a halfway point for us.

We met on our two month mark at a great hotel in downtown Columbia. I changed clothing about five times, and finally I arrived at the hotel. I pulled up in front, spied Stone, and I jumped out of the car. Unfortunately, I was in the road and not in the valet part. Luckily, the valet guy laughed and took my keys.

Stone laughed and shook his head. "Oh my God! That's something my wife would have done."

At last, we entered into our incredible room and were ready to have a blast. The hotel was originally a bank. The bar in the hotel was located in the vault. We walked down to the vault and toasted each other.

"This is such a cool hotel, Maddie, and I'm so happy we're together. Although I am a little worried about your parking ability."

"Listen, I was so excited when I saw you, I thought I was in the valet aisle. I was counting the hours waiting for this weekend. Here's to us. You make me so happy, Stone."

We walked around the streets of Columbia and eventually found a great little Mexican place where we experienced a fabulous meal. Like young lovers, we were glued to each other and couldn't stop smiling throughout dinner.

Back at the hotel, my guy and I enjoyed a very romantic night. While Stone went to get ice, I lit a zillion candles around the room, and the fresh scent of the vanilla bean candles wafted throughout adding to the ambience of the evening.

He opened the door, looked around the room, and smiled. "Of course you brought candles, and I just happened to bring my speaker. We sure think along the same lines, baby."

"Stone, I'm over the top for you. Whenever I think our time together can't get any better, it does! You're the sweetest most romantic guy on my planet."

The weekend ended way too fast, and our great time together confirmed this guy was for me. I hated to go back home and to the endless routine of phone calls and plans.

Chapter 16

In the fall, hurricane season blows its way into coastal South Carolina through the end of November. As it turned out, this year proved to be no different.

Stone needed to take a trip to Colorado for hand surgery which included a short week with one of his best friends. I worked very hard and kept my eye on the weather forecast which changed every hour. Most of my park decided to evacuate away from the beach. All this uncertainty made me a bit nervous and unsure as to what to do. My son would be fine and planned to have his father stay with him.

I texted Stone, "Hey baby, this storm has your girl a bit worried. I'm thinking about driving up to your house to ride it out. I know you're still in Colorado, but at least I can be in a place that makes me very happy."

"Of course, you can stay in my house, babe. That would make me happy to know you're there. And I have some good news for you. My buddy needs to get back to the coast to help with his older family. I'm coming home, too. We can ride out the hurricane safely in the mountains."

"Nothing would make me happier than to be with you, Stone. I'm planning on leaving sometime tomorrow, but I don't know how crazy it'll be driving out of South Carolina. I'll keep you posted. I love you. Fly safely!"

Due to the uncertainty of the storm situation, I was unsure of how much I needed to pack. Would there be a home to come back to? Would I still have a job? My job entailed working in a manufactured home park with tons of trees. I left the next morning, and it was so eerie as no one was coming into the beach. The governor had ordered the highways be reversed heading out of town, but very few cars traveled on the road thus far. This whole situation felt scary and surreal as I headed to the mountains.

I arrived at Stone's a few hours after he'd returned to his house. Relief and relaxation swept through me knowing I was now safe and secure. We had the Weather Channel on, and the situation looked pretty bleak.

The next day, the storm turned a bit, but flooding became the huge problem along with the wind. I called my friends, and they all said the same thing, "Oh my God! The flooding and the wind are terrible!" Tons of trees limbs had fallen, and all the canals overflowed. South Carolina was declared a state of emergency, and no one was allowed back into the state. But everyone I knew was safe, and for that I was grateful.

I realized with the roads closed, I'd just received a mountain vacation I hadn't planned on. Spending a week here was a gift, and it only reinforced how much I wanted this man in my life. Every day we planned our menu and had some fabulous dinners. We spent time watching shows on Netflix. Every night Stone made me a raging fire, while we sipped our wine. I loved sitting in front of the fireplace stunned by all that was happening between us. My little mountain vacation was just perfect. And we had a playlist of our special songs and even danced in the kitchen. I could have lived in those magical moments forever.

Chapter 17

Unfortunately, all good things must come to an end. South Carolina looked like it was opening back up. I had a window of time in which I needed to get back to the beach. Getting closer to my state, made me feel more nervous as there was no way of knowing what the area looked like due to the flooding. I spoke with Stone a lot on my way home. He was very concerned.

Finally, as I approached closer to my area, I gave him a call with good news. "Hey babe, I'm about thirty minutes from home, and all is well."

"Oh thank God! I was getting so worried. You just take your time, and you'll be home before you know it. I already miss you. I love you. Call me when you get unpacked."

I no sooner ended that call when I noticed a road block and a detour miles long. It had started to get dark, and because I don't see very well at night, I began to panic. Directions aren't my thing, and there's a detour to where? Would I know how to get home? I followed the long line of cars and kept looking at my gas tank, hoping I wouldn't need gas as no place was open. Totally dark now, fear crept in. I pulled into a gas station near Georgetown, and all the roads were closed. Three older men stood around in the gas station, but there was no gas.

I asked, "Do y'all know if roads are washed out?"

"You must be going to Pawley's Island with that Mercedes," one guy joked.

One of the other men said, "Take this road down about five miles. Then take the next two left turns from there. But be careful. There are spots of flooding just about everywhere."

The third man chimed in as I was about to drive away. "Yes, you be careful young lady! They say snakes and gators are on the roads, too!"

"Okay. Well, thank you so much for the directions." Oh great! The last thing I wanted was to have my car stall out by the river. And snakes and gators? Yikes! I was now more of a wreck than before.

I drove the winding dark roads on the center line. There wasn't a car on the road. Water flooded on both sides, so I continued to drive right down the middle in the ink black night. I trembled, and my heart pounded. I thought, what if those men had told me the wrong way? Finally, the road ended, and there was the turn they'd told me about. I turned and saw the main road which still overflowed with water, but I knew my location. I was on Highway 17 headed to Pawleys Island. Lanes of the highway were closed, but oh my God, I kept my cool and kept driving very slowly until I got to higher ground.

The rest of the way was much better. I arrived at my home nine hours from when I'd started, and the drive is usually 5 and a half hours. Still shaking, I pulled into my parking lot and just cried with relief. Thank God, I'd made it home! The ride had been awful, but I'd do it all again to have had that week in the mountains. That nightmarish experience was worth it all!

Chapter 18

Stone and I had a few weeks before Thanksgiving which would be our first big holiday together. We were lucky to have spent a whole week with each other due to the hurricane but were so excited to be celebrating this special occasion together. Stone's sister was hosting Thanksgiving dinner at her home, and I couldn't wait to see his family again. My son would spend the holiday with his dad, so I was off to Asheville for a four day vacation!

Thanksgiving was a fabulous time. Stone's sister's home provided the perfect place for a huge family dinner and accommodated all twenty of us. The dinner was amazing, but before we dined, everyone held hands and prayed. I glanced around the enormous table and thought how wonderful was this family!

I loved every single minute of this weekend. On Friday, we visited the wonderful Gingerbread festival at Grove Park Inn. I was so excited to see the spectacular fall colors as we drove through the mountains. Later, I sat at the table with Stone's mom. What a gracious and fun person to be around.

In December, Stone was going away for Christmas with his daughters, his brother and sister- in- law. The trip had been planned for months. It was funny because the first night we'd met, Stone told me he didn't know if we would be dating then, but he had plans to be away at Christmas. I had thought, wow! You're telling me this on our first date? So now I told him, "When you get to Abaco Island, you'd better send your girl flowers for Christmas." Hah! He was so damned sweet.

Another getaway was planned in Columbia before he left for his trip. We met for two days, and our time there was just as great as the last rendezvous. But a weird vibe surrounded us because of his leaving for Christmas. Neither one of us had anticipated this would happen. I finally found this incredible guy, and he was going away over Christmas! We clung to each other a little tighter as we said our goodbyes. I was also sad because he told me the reception where he'd be would be spotty, and so we probably wouldn't be able to talk much. So, not only would he be gone all week, but we'd hardly have any chance to talk.

To keep my mind off Stone, I worked extra hard, kept busy, and went out with the girls for some drinks. On Christmas Eve, I came home in the late afternoon, and to my surprise, there was a beautiful bouquet of white tulips tied together with a Christmas bow along with a great card. Stone had nailed it, remembering my favorite flower. What blew me away was, even though he was getting ready for a trip to a tropical paradise and with all the craziness that entailed, he still went to a florist and made sure these gorgeous flowers would arrive on Christmas Eve! So incredibly happy, I just danced around the house!

But the best thing was when he called me on Christmas Day, and we talked for a few minutes. My phone rang, and there was that *magnificent voice*! "Merry Christmas, baby. How's my favorite girl?"

"Well, considering I just received a beautiful arrangements of tulips, I'd say pretty happy, baby. They're just beautiful and so hard to find this time of year. I feel very loved."

"You are very loved by me, Maddie. I wish you could be here to see this place. It's beautiful. The weather isn't so great, though. It's actually chilly, and of course, I didn't pack correctly. I have shorts and bathing suits and nothing even remotely warm."

"Why, oh why, doesn't that surprise me? But maybe it'll turn warmer in a day or two."

"Nope. The forecast has changed, and it's downright cold. We rented a boat, but the water's way too choppy. No one wants to even go near the boat! I even bribed my daughters to come in the boat, but there were no takers."

"Stone, you are too funny. Only you would be a

vacation dressed for the wrong season. You're so dam cute, and I can only imagine what it must be like."

"The house is really great. We've found a few places to go for dinner, but of course, riding to them in the golf cart is not too warm. We'll be playing cards and staying inside most nights. There's a cool tree house on the property, and I think I'll stay there. It has a comfortable bed and a small kitchen. The best part, though, is there's Wi-Fi, and I'll be able to call you every single night! I miss you so much, Maddie."

"Baby, you just made my Christmas. You never cease to amaze me. I was so bummed and sad that we wouldn't be able to talk. Now, I'm ecstatic, and it will feel like I'm with you. I miss you more than you can imagine. We've been together for six months now, and I can't imagine my life without you."

We talked for hours every night, and Stone had me in stitches about his exploits during the day. We got through the week, and we made plans to spend New Year's at the beach.

Stone's family condo was open, and we spent the most incredibly romantic week together. This amazing man and I walked on the beach every day, sat on the porch drinking wine, and listened to the Atlantic Ocean roaring to the shore. We slept with the windows open with the sea lulling us to sleep. I never wanted the week to end!

Chapter 19

The holidays were over, and Stone and I had spent a great deal of time together. We were looking forward to the adventures the new year would bring.

January ended up being a busy month, and we did see each other about every two weeks. The next big event we planned was Valentine's Day weekend. This was our very first Valentine's Day, and Stone didn't disappoint.

We planned to spend one night at the Grove Park Inn and get massages the next day. I drove up after work, but before driving to the inn, we went over to visit his mom for a while. Next, Stone and I were off to the hotel which was only about a mile and a half from his house.

We walked into a room, and wow! What an incredible view, and the room was equally exquisite. But the surprises from Stone were even better. A vase of white tulips graced a table, and chocolate covered strawberries were placed next to the flowers. There was also a cooler with a few bottles of our favorite wine.

Then, unexpectedly, a bottle of wine was delivered from his best friend. I was stunned. This was perfection…the most romantic day, with the most romantic guy, in the most romantic place. Stone and I enjoyed a nice dinner in front of the enormous fireplace. In the background, we heard someone playing beautiful piano music. What a night to remember!

The next day we'd be going to the spa at Grove Park. After a quick breakfast, Stone and I entered into the underground spa. The incredible scents of eucalyptus, coconut and vanilla wafted through the air. We donned our robes and slippers and sat in front of the fire sipping water. Our treatments were separate; mine was a hot stone, and his was a deep tissue. Fabulous! Next, we met in the couple's room and were led to the pool. Nothing compared to this place: five pools, waterfalls, and salt water. The lights and colors were amazing! We spent the whole day enjoying this world renowned underground spa. As the day wound down, we went outside to the spa's huge outdoor hot tub. The water was bubbling hot, and a few other couples also enjoyed this luxury. We drifted to the side, and a waiter brought us champagne. I looked up at the sky full of stars, and all of the sudden, it started snowing! The snowflakes, the sky, the bubbling hot tub, the champagne, and this guy…oh my God! What could ever be better? Our first Valentine's Day could only be described as something out of a fairytale.

Chapter 20

Our lives at this point entwined like vines of ivy. Stone and I texted all day, talked on the phone every night, and planned and dreamed all the time.

April was my birthday, and we decided to go to Bald Head Island, North Carolina, which would surely be another fantastic adventure. We journeyed to Wilmington to visit his friend and dined in a place called Blue Water.

Before dinner, I changed into a really pretty top I'd bought for the trip. "Hey baby, what do you think ? Do you like this top ? I want to look great when I meet your best friend."

With his beautiful blue eyes, Stone scanned me up and down. "Hmm…as usual you look gorgeous, but it looks like you're missing something."

Slowly, he came up behind me and opened a blue box. Then, my love proceeded to put a diamond necklace around my neck.

He kissed me tenderly. "There, that looks much better my hottie."

I stood there speechless for a few seconds, and my eyes teared up. "Oh baby, I just love it! I can't believe you just gave this to me. You took me away for an incredible weekend, but I never expected this, Stone! I just love you so much, my silly man."

We had such a lovely time celebrating my birthday. There was nothing like spending a night in a hotel; it's always fun and brings out the best in both of us.

Early in the morning, we drove to Southport. The short ferry ride to Bald Head Island was made all the more romantic by the haunting cries of following seagulls. The view of the stunning homes took our breaths away as we pulled into the incredibly scenic harbor. Everything was whitewashed or light gray weathered by the ocean. Once on Bald Head, we took a shuttle to the beautiful bed and breakfast called the Inn at Bald Head.

Stone and I arrived at the a lovely, white, beach style building with wide wooden steps. It was impossible to miss the baskets of hanging flowers and the pretty flower boxes on every window. This quaint inn featured a bed and breakfast with six rooms. Our fantastic room included a private bath and a great little porch overlooking the Atlantic Ocean. The inn served a great breakfast with croissants, fresh fruit, muffins, mimosas, and cereals. A huge living room stunned us with its warm ambiance as the morning sun radiated throughout the room.

After breakfast we rented a golf cart since there were no cars on the island. My guy and I had the best time driving around and noticed the golf course and miles of amazing beaches.

At happy hour, the inn hosted a delightful array of heavy hors d' oeuvres and wine. My love and I took our drinks and sat on the rocking chairs overlooking the panoramic harbor. Our day continued with a great dinner at Mojos, and then we held hands all the way back to the phenomenal Bald Head Island Inn. Finally, Stone and I completed celebrating my romantic birthday weekend by listening to our music and enjoying wine…a birthday which would forever stay in my memory.

Chapter 21

The months flew by, and I became quite a fixture in Asheville. The area simply drew me in with Stone's fun and loving family, his gorgeous house, and the stunning views.

His mom and I saw a lot of each other, and I always made a point to drop off a book and anything chocolate. Every time I walked into her home, she would get out of her chair, say my name, and greet me with a huge smile and a big hug. I loved being around her, and she seemed to love seeing her son and me together.

One day I did something unique but never mentioned it to Stone. There's a sweet little bookstore in Pawleys Island called Litchfield Books. This quaint shop had all the newest books and unique gifts for special occasions. It also had wonderful gifts for writers. I could spend hours in this shop.

At that particular moment in time, I happened to be in the area and wanted to send his mom a book. When I walked into the bookstore, there was a book signing going on. Imagine my surprise when I saw my favorite author, Mary Alice Monroe, sitting behind a huge stack of books. Thrilled, I grabbed two copies of her new book and had both signed. I wanted this famous author to inscribe something personal for Stone's mom, but I didn't know for sure what to say. I told Mary Alice Monroe a little bit about Mrs. Stone, and it was apparent how important she'd become in my life. She smiled, picked up her pen, and wrote, *To the matriarch of a beautiful family… Love, Mary Alice Monroe.* I thanked her profusely, and then bought a huge chocolate bar. Immediately, I mailed these special gifts to Stone's lovely mother.

Two days later, Stone called, "Hey mom just called and said she received a parcel in the mail. It was a book and also a chocolate bar. Did you send her something?"

I burst into laughter. "Yeah, I sure did. I wanted to surprise her. It's a beach story, and inside she wrote something to your mom. Make sure you look at the inscription."

"I'll make sure mom sees it. Baby, that was so thoughtful of you to do. You made my mom so happy. She's probably told everyone in Asheville about her parcel."

In July, the whole family would vacation at the beach near where I lived, and this year I'd join them. Although I eagerly anticipated this family event, it would be the first time I'd be meeting his daughters from Kentucky, and that truly worried me. I'd met all his brothers, sisters, and most of the cousins, but meeting his daughters was a whole different story. Stone and I had dated a whole year, but due to geography and work, we'd never met before. Stone had met my son at the beach and had actually golfed with him. They hit it off immediately. But with his daughters, I pondered as to how it would all work out. I worried his girls wouldn't like me. After losing their mom, how would they take to their dad's girlfriend who appeared to not be going away?

This traditional beach week occurred yearly and had been in full force the actual week I'd met Stone. Nothing really prepared me for this special event. The week overflowed with family, dinners, love, and laughter. We rented a house with his sister, and it was explained to each of us that we'd take a turn of preparing dinner for the whole group of thirty-nine. Our night of cooking would be Wednesday. Oh great! I hate to cook, and now I had to create a dinner for this many.

His sister had the first night of cooking dinner at the house we'd rented together. After work, while driving to "our" house, I became a bundle of nerves knowing Stone's oldest daughter would be there. His sisters reassured me as they knew how I felt.

Stone drove the golf cart to pick up his mom and daughter. I stood in the kitchen, and the basement door opened. I remembered swallowing and thinking oh, I hope it goes well. In walked Stone's mom with his daughter following. Flashing a huge smile, his mom hugged me tightly. I sensed his daughter to be quite surprised that I not only had a relationship with her grandmother but his siblings, too. I gave her a hug and noticed she wore a red shorts outfit with a little jacket. This young lady was a stunning and classy knockout, and I loved how she wore her hair pulled back in a bun. After a few moments, she joined all the cousins.

After a fabulous dinner, the night progressed, and the drinks flowed freely. Stone's daughter and I finally had a chance to talk. She and I sized each other up, and I felt everything would be okay. Of course, things were tentative, but we had the whole week to become more acquainted.

Stone's other stunning daughter arrived the next day. She smiled, and we talked a bit about her job and her life.

The whole family spent all week together, enjoying days on the gorgeous beach and every night feasting on fabulous dinners. Spending so much time together definitely helped to break the ice. Although the situation was fresh between us all, I believed Stone's daughters saw their dad as a happy man.

This had been my first beach week, and I not only survived it but loved every second being with this family.

Chapter 22

After beach week, our life together seemed perfect. Stone and I still continued to see each other every two weeks, and our relationship grew stronger. His beautiful daughters were happy their dad was in a good place. We decided to take things slowly, so that all of our children felt comfortable with the developing relationship between their parents.

The time finally came to plan a trip to Kentucky where Stone used to live and where his daughters still lived. We planned on arriving on Thanksgiving weekend. Filled with excitement and anticipation, I planned and shopped. But then, some unfortunate news took the wind from my sails.

My ex-husband had been taken to the hospital with pneumonia. He'd battled with his health for a while now suffering from COPD, breathing issues, and also prostate cancer. Arriving at the hospital, I quickly realized the severity of his illnesses. Stunned to see him hooked up to tubes, I knew I couldn't leave my ex while his health failed. I couldn't leave my only son there alone to face this terrible situation, and I knew he'd be scared to death.

So, I stayed home, and a few days later my ex-husband died in the hospital. But my heart broke for my poor twenty-eight year old son, whose father had died while he'd stayed right by his side. I think that life works out in the end. My son's father could have died in a car or at home alone. My son and his girlfriend were always busy and traveled often. They could have been away when his dad went to the hospital. As it turned out, they were right near the hospital, and my son was able to hold his father's hand. They expressed many things to each other including my son's thank you for the brand new home which I knew his father had built for him. Orchestrated perfectly, all the loose ends were tied in a bow. Nothing is ever random. I thank God every day that he got closure, and that the last thing his dad saw before he passed away was our son's face.

Thanksgiving certainly wasn't what any of us had planned. Stone went to Kentucky alone and spent time with his girls. And for that I was thankful.

Chapter 23

I continued working hard trying to get the numbers for the year. Stone and I had planned for me to go to his home for Christmas as my son would spend the holiday with his girl's family. So, our Christmas together was quiet and beautiful.

For New Year's, we traveled to Kentucky to spend time with his daughters. I'd never been to Kentucky, and I delighted in its beauty. The countryside of horse farms stunned us with its abundance of black barns and black fencing.

Stone's oldest daughter hosted an amazing party at her home. Beautifully decorated, the ambiance and the food were wonderful, and many family and friends showed up.

Stone and I stayed with his other daughter, and she made us feel welcomed as we enjoyed the perfect pleasure of her guest room. Both of his girls offered kind courtesy, and I felt acceptance. Stone had been right;

proceed slowly with all of our kids.

Time flew by, and I visited Asheville often. We also stayed in Litchfield at his family's amazing condo. We bounced back and forth between our two places. Winter at the beach is a gift. There are no crowds, no traffic, and it's just peaceful. This year, Stone and I celebrated Valentine's Day in Hilton Head, South Carolina, and we enjoyed two incredible nights of fabulous dinners and a massage.

Our routine worked out great for us and we saw each other every two weeks. Our fairytale romance continued, and we visited many spectacular places. In the spring, we explored Chimney Rock and Lake Lure. My great mountain man and I packed picnics and went to the fabulous Biltmore. Every month unfolded into another exciting adventure.

One weekend, we drove to his sister's beautiful mountain house which easily could have been in a movie. A massive front porch greeted us, and a scattering of quaint rocking chairs allowed us a place to sit and contemplate life for a while. Stone and I enjoyed the Fourth of July at Grove Park Inn, and the fireworks were absolutely stunning! And just like that it, beach week arrived again.

Chapter 24

Another incredible week arrived with this amazing family. Golf-carts, beach time, and dinners were the order of the day. We rented a house with Stone's sister which resulted in absolute craziness. Every night the party ended up in this house. Our special time together provided so much laughter and at the helm was the beautiful proud matriarch.

This regal and elegant lady watched in awe this family she'd created. Her grandchildren loved her, and she forever wore a happy smile on her face. Mrs. Stone walked to the beach every morning and read while sitting in her favorite chair every afternoon. In the late afternoon, she loved coming down to the beach to observe everyone having so much fun. There were tents, coolers, and way too many happy people. The last night, Mrs. Stone always took the entire family out for dinner. What wonderful memories to treasure forever.

In the fall, Stone noticed his mom wasn't eating much, and thus had lost weight. She also slept more than usual. At eighty-nine, that was pretty much expected, but still, Stone worried. The family all got together and set up doctor appointments for her.

In the meantime, a family wedding had been planned for the day after Thanksgiving. Due to the pandemic, the wedding date changed a few times. Everyone hoped Mrs. Stone would be able to attend the wedding. This beautiful family all rallied, and every single grandchild came up to see and spend time with her. Stone's sisters and brother took turns staying at the house. Each week her energy seemed to dissipate, and her doctors determined she had cancer.

At first, Mrs. Stone still sat in her special chair. But eventually, this sweet lady started staying in bed more and more, and we'd all sit with her to keep her company.

A day I will always remember was when hospice came. Since the pandemic, someone coming to the house from hospice had proved to be difficult. Stone's sister had a friend who was a nurse, and she came over to give Mrs. Stone a shower. Stone and his sister heated up the walk in-shower, and while she showered, we all grabbed new soft pajamas and stripped the bed. Then, we made up her bed with new sheets and a brand new comforter found in a closet. Mrs. Stone sunk into a cloud of a bed all clean and warm. She grabbed the comforter and said, "Oh, how soft. Where did you get this wonderful comforter?" Seeing her so comfortable and warm made me so happy.

The next few days were a blur, but we knew Mrs. Stone's life was coming to an end. She slept all the time.

Stone and I went in to see her, and as we tiptoed in, she opened her eyes and smiled. "Where are you two going?"

Stone replied, "Mama, we're not going anywhere. We're here with you."

Those were the last words she said to us.

That night, Stone's brother- in- law said a rosary at her bedside. Everyone went in and said the rosary with him. What a beautiful moment. This amazing woman, in the middle of a pandemic, rested in her own bed surrounded by all of her praying children. After the rosary, we all chatted, and I'm sure she heard nothing but laughter and felt an abundance of love radiating in that room. Mrs. Stone died peacefully that night. Again, I say nothing is ever random. This lovely lady raised six kids, and what a gift to take your last breath surrounded by all your loving family. I loved her!

Mrs. Stone died early in November, and thus was unable to see her granddaughter get married. The wedding occurred after Thanksgiving, and her home held Thanksgiving for us all. I know she would have loved that.

In the middle of Covid, the wedding went on without a hitch. This special event took place in an outdoor tent venue on a spectacular day. The wedding happened on the last date it could have been held. The guests wore masks to err on the side of caution. Over a hundred people attended the wedding, and not one of them contacted Covid. We liked to think Mrs. Stone gave us a beautiful day and kept us all safe.

Chapter 25

After Stone's mom died, I knew he struggled as they'd shared such a strong relationship. His mother often told me she didn't want him sitting in his chair watching TV alone. This lovely woman and I enjoyed many conversations, and she knew how much I loved her son.

Whenever I needed to leave to go back to work, she'd sweetly say, "Just stay. If you're waiting for my blessing, you had it the day you walked in this house." I pondered her words after she died and thought again how short life was.

I surely had a great job and made great money, but working during the pandemic changed all that for me. Showing homes to people from out of state made me fearful, and sanitizing everything in sight was no fun. I thought long and hard about life. This wonderful man who I thought I'd never find had entered my life. Stone and I had discussed about me moving to Asheville. Many hours were spent walking on the beach and thinking about our future. Finally, I called him. We discussed the importance of my moving up right before Christmas. So, I walked away from a career and the place I'd called home for the last 13 years. My decision was huge, but my son was on board. I also decided to keep my place in Murrells Inlet, SC.

On December 19th, I drove up the mountain with a car full of clothes and everything important. When I finally arrived at his house, Stone wrapped his arms around me and said, "Welcome home."

That night, he made a fabulous dinner and lit a fire. The atmosphere felt very surreal.

The next morning, feeling like a princess, I awoke to coffee brought to me in bed. This was the start of my new life. In the kitchen, I looked out the window, and to my surprise, it was snowing. And right there in the driveway were a mama bear and four cubs! Such is my mountain life!

This past year has been a gift. I've pretty much walked everyday up these beautiful mountains and explored so many fantastic places. I've hiked up Grandfather Mountain, crossed the swinging bridge, and viewed breathtaking waterfalls. Stone and I remodeled two bathrooms and added a lot of touches to his home.

I sat looking out his window at the mountains with a book in my hands and felt the warmth of the stone fireplace. In the backdrop a steady hand held mine. I have had so much laughter and tenderness.

Last summer, we visited Grove Park Inn and had a drink on the terrace. Stone asked if I were cold. He proceeded to go inside, but instead he got down on his knee with a box in his hand. This wonderful man opened the box, and a light shined down on the most beautiful ring I've ever seen. "Maddie, will you marry me?"

We planned to get married very quietly. Somehow, I thought, a beach, a sunset, and a pretty sky were all that would be needed!

Epilogue

July 6, 2022

After almost four years to the day of meeting, Stone and I exchanged our wedding vows in an absolutely beautiful ceremony. We'd become engaged in the mountains, so we married at the beach... the best of both worlds!

We wanted our ceremony to be private and special. Fortunately, we found a woman who performed beach weddings. We grabbed a bouquet of white tulips, ordered a huge cupcake to use as our wedding cake, and purchased a bottle of champagne. Our exquisite wedding ceremony was performed at the beach access of Media Road in North Litchfield, South Carolina. Stone and I climbed to the top of the weathered wooden platform, and all we saw was a beautiful empty beach, a stunning sunset, and each other.

CPSIA information can be obtained
at www.ICGtesting.com
Printed in the USA
LVHW100329170123
737236LV00006BA/223

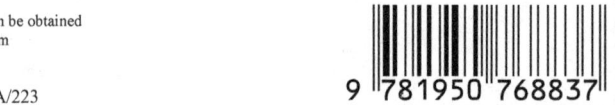